INSIDE THE WALLS

INSIDE THE WALLS

EMERY E. FINCH

Pine Nest Press

Content Warning:
Imagery and topics (violence/death/sexual themes) that may be disturbing to readers.

A character within this story uses they/them pronouns. While they may not be familiar or traditional to some, the author intentionally chose to use them.

I.

"...and that's our September Seven, seven top songs falling into your speakers like leaves outside. A chill is coming into East Barkerfield tonight and won't leave for a week—so grab your radio and bundle up with us, here on 89.4..."

Garbling static squealed in time with the tires along the road. A tin beat pulsing and popping in speakers long blown out, an auto-tuned melody, churning gravel; they all heaved in harmony as the car rumbled. The chorus played in vibrations against the window and rattled against my cheek.

I brought my arm up to act as a pillow again, propping my chin upon my jacket to watch the never-ending fields wave to me. I had seen the soybean shore at least an hour before, but we were still driving in an ocean—and had yet to pass a sign of any life at all. Maybe it would be worthwhile to ask if they were lost—but breaking the suspended silence came at a price.

The radio scratched into a new song.

"Don't you have something else, *Avie*?" A palm came to smack the radio into clarity, but the signal failed to improve. The nickname seemed to drag on longer than the pitched notes of the songs. She playfully lifted her voice with her shoulders, leaning up on her elbows to crane into the driver's space and give a dramatic pout. Hallie was good at pouting, but it never lasted; they all were too used to the tactic. "C'mon, I hate this station, let's listen to something else."

A practiced hand reached from behind the wheel to pinch her cheek between a thumb and index finger until Hallie leaned back again.

"CD player's broken, *duck*."

Avie. Duck. The nicknames were getting worse. I scrunched my nose at the window. The glass hit my temple with every bump in the dirt, but it was still better than sitting upright. If I moved an inch forward, I'd be in sight of the rearview mirror—and I didn't want to see the reflection of brown eyes staring back.

Shoved between the cracked car door and the mountain of equipment, forced to look at farms or steal glances at Hallie in the passenger seat, was arguably the best position for the time being. There, I could see Hallie's profile, huddled over the window and resting her head against the glass. The afternoon sun treated her kindly. It reflected off a chain of crystals dangling from the mirror and splayed onto her chest in prisms of reds, greens, and oranges. It glittered on her necklace too, a silver line like a scar on her collar, and dripped stars with every movement she made. When she shifted back into her seat, when she swatted Avery's hand away— when her chest inflated with laughter.

Her fingers came to examine the ends of her hair while she giggled away the last of Avery's attention. Maybe she checked for damage from her last box dye job, black, she had insisted in the pharmacy aisles. This time was important, she needed to dress for her role in our newest adventure.

Let me pay you. Let me buy you takeout. I'll spoil you to a movie night, come watch the next horror movie that comes out in theaters. I'll do yours next.

Hallie had offered so much in exchange for long hours over a chipped bathroom sink and inescapable fumes scratching at our lungs, but I refused. Instead, I watched her giggle over dye stains and try to wash them from her hands. Her fingers had been soft when they turned over my palms to scrub at the splotches.

I glanced down at my lap.

"Why didn't you fix it before we came out here?" Hallie sighed and fiddled with the visor. "Once we're famous, get a new car, okay? This one is past dead."

"How about you pay for it then?" Avery retorted with a twist of their hands on the wheel. It was an old game they played, back-and-forth insults toward the vehicle. It puttered along at fourteen years old, albeit with leaks and questionable functionality. But, it was all they had, and without it, they wouldn't be on their way to the house.

I settled farther into my home against the tired leather of the backseat. I knew each crack and tear in the lining and peeling finish of the window ledge. I had memorized the way the highway kissed the fields and the press of equipment bags piled against the outer seam of my jeans. From here, everyone had become a familiar sight. Hallie's profile from the passenger seat. Avery's spiked hair peeked out from the headrest. Blake's nonexistence—save for the occasional beep or tap as he tinkered away with his laptop. Every so often, he'd pop up to rummage for a snack, messy brown bangs in his eyes, and give me a little nod.

We held a backseat alliance. He would do his quiet typing on a keyboard for a while, zip the duffel bags here and there, and offer me a couple of chips or half a sandwich. I would trade him books or doodles of imagined billboards that seemed best suited for the rural roads we always seemed to explore.

The radio was ignored as Hallie breathed out a loud sigh. She opened her book again.

I shifted my legs, pressing them together to keep my activities balanced. An empty notebook and pen wavered between my knees, held up by a bridge of folded newspaper. The article, I read six times; I was meant to use it as inspiration. However, I had learned long ago that it was like an unexpected dinner guest; arriving too late or too early and forcing the host to accommodate on short notice.

I played a game with myself, to keep the lull of passing soy and rumbling highway at bay. I would pick up my pen and spin it once, flick it against the paper, and set it down again. Then again. I'd listen to whatever mumbling faded in and out of static on the radio. I'd note Avery's constant retorts. Watch Hallie's fingers turn the pages of her book. Then, I'd look at the lines of my notebook and wait.

I had never won this game. The page was blank.

Gravel kicked against the deflated back wheel of the sedan like a sputtering criminal in a courtroom, pleading for a verdict. This was it, our judgment—and yet, the drive to the investigation was like any other. Our fate was held in the decrepit walls of an abandoned house. Everything else had been unsuccessful. We couldn't get enough evidence or views on our videos online. My zines didn't sell. Newspapers wouldn't pick up the articles I submitted. We had exhausted every "haunted" house in our town, then our county, and somehow, never came up with the same evidence the other investigators did. Six months of nothing—and now, the decision arose. Was it worth the called-off part-time jobs, the scraped funding for barren investigations– or the time owed to "real work"?

Real work. What a joke. Stuck in an office or store doing something meaningless and exploitative didn't seem like "real work"—even if this investigation failed, it was more meaningful than a shift at some gray corporation.

I lifted my head from the window and thumbed at the newspaper in my lap, tugging it out enough to read the headline for the seventh time.

Killer Ghost or Ghostly Killer? Amateur Investigators Found Dead in Local Haunt

Two ghost hunters, a local couple in their thirties who ran a prominent blog online, decided to investigate a farmhouse. Said farmhouse, authorities quoted, had not seen residents in nearly a century. Abandoned after being built. The couple received permission from authorities to stay overnight and never emerged alive. When the medics arrived, one was found with no wounds in a bedroom, the other face down in the bathtub—and the doors were locked from the inside. The nearest neighbor lived four miles away.

The story was too vague.

I could feel my skin itch every time I scanned the page. The journalist covering the piece wrote it with the same simple prose as a report on new corporate construction. There was no creative description to differentiate the author's voice from a robotic spew akin to a teleprompter– I would have made the descriptions vivid. *Emotional. Frightening*– enough to earn my place on the evening news interviews and write an exposé on the nuance of haunting and the misconception of popular bloggers.

The journalist had two interviews, one in the evening and one before the police's debrief. I watched them all with Blake, a limp slice of pizza in hand and eyes glued to the spitting upper lip of the police chief. She concluded with no danger in the area and they turned on each other. The friends and family of the pair disagreed, with a sister commenting how out of character it was. Before I could repeat her and look to Blake, he had already flipped his phone on and furiously tapped a message to Avery.

The parents of the investigators were offering rewards for information. *Any* information. News outlets built anticipation and offered interviews for any new leads. Nothing like this happened in their county, nothing so ominous happened in the vast fields—it was the happenings of a horror movie. Other local crews had been gathering up their resources to investigate the farmhouse themselves, but all had been too nervous to go first.

What did they have to lose?

Avery wanted to do it immediately, but they wanted to do *everything* immediately. Loud, bold, and brave. Avery would take any opportunity to copy what they saw on television shows, talk channels, and hunting blogs—it was an insatiable obsession. No matter the danger or apprehension, it would be impossible to pull them away. Like pulling a hound from blood, we could do nothing but watch them arrive at my bedroom door, palm pressed into the frame and eyes blown wide with a fresh whiff of potential fame.

Hallie didn't seem to be nervous either. She had heard the deaths and took her time arriving. When she did, she shrugged her shoulders, claiming the fated pair were probably not doing their seance properly. Or their prayers. Or called upon the correct guidance. Each new flaw brought another glint to her eye as she crowded herself into the bedroom that night. Her interests were like Avery's; obsessive. Though, while they focused on hunting the ghosts, she fixated on ways to rid them. Her long rants of exorcism and proper religious practice were perfected with each car ride, but I never really minded. She could say the grass was meant to be pink or humans were born on another planet and shipped here in long spaceships; I would continue not to mind. She always said something thought-provoking. About exorcism, one day. The morals of humans and demons, the next. If fallen angels would be included in the concept of predestination. Free will. She was always quoting documentaries and essays she had written in her undergraduate program, but never rubbed her education in our faces— Avery was not as humble. They boasted their progression at community college like a parrot when presented with attention.

It was a shame Avery and Hallie liked each other so much. *Just friends*, they promised Blake and me, but seeing them joke with each other with those brief arm touches yanked at my stomach. Or when Hallie praised Avery for finishing certificates like that *meant* something—or when Avery called her duck and pinched her lips. *Or. Or. Or.* There were too many examples, and each one tasted like bile.

"Are you reading that again?" The duffel bags beside my hip shifted and Blake peeked over the handles. He tucked the end of his mousy hair behind his ear, but it fell back against his retreating fingers. He never mastered styling it. "You'll freak yourself out."

"I already read it. Reading it again won't change anything." I let my eyes roll, shifting it under the notebook again. Blake didn't make any move to return to his typing. "What, you scared? Still?"

"People died," Blake mumbled as he sat back. His fingernails picked at a torn thread in his sweatshirt. "I just think it could be a bad idea."

"You texted Avery first, you know." Reminding him felt unfair. He had been nervous since we packed the car at Avery's apartment.

"If we get this on tape, we'll be famous. It's worth it." Avery called back from their seat. "Don't freak out, Blake, we're good. You'll be in a tech room anyway, I won't even make you solo an EVP."

"Lucky me." Blake hushed under his breath. He closed his laptop and shoved it in a backpack next to his feet, rustling around to escape the conversation.

"It'll be fine in the base we make," I promised with a pat on the duffel bags. From above the canvas straps, I could see him continue to pick at what remained of his short nails. "We need this investigation, anyway. Just stay with Hal if you get scared."

Hallie turned in her seat to grin at Blake, waving her

fingers in a fluid wiggle. "I'll protect you from the ghosts, got my bible ready."

"What are you going to do, beat them with it?"

"Exactly." Hallie lifted the book in her lap and made a mock swing. "Smack them back to the other side."

"And what if we find out the other team was murdered by something else? Something worse than a ghost?"

"Then," Avery glanced back in the mirror. I met their gaze. "We kick a not-ghosts's ass. Claire is going to write a killer article about how the mystery has been solved. We get famous. We keep investigating."

My eyes lowered again to the pen resting on the blank notebook. *It was that simple, wasn't it?*

The car slowed and pulled into a winding drive, weaving into the space between two dead fields. The farmhouse peeked out from the overgrowth and my hand wound the window crank with a dizzying spin. Within seconds of hitting the driveway, I was unbuckled and leaning through the door to squint at our savior.

A simple, plain square greeted us with chipping paint and cracked glass between the broken shutters on the second floor. There was an attempt to board one up from within, haphazard and uneven planks thrown on in haste. Maintenance escaped the house, leaving the shingles clustered like loose teeth. They smiled at us while the tires crushed grass beneath their tracks and rumbled to a stop.

A Midwestern farmhouse, no different than the hundreds that dotted the lone highways and farms across the region. Sprouted from the earth with a lone tree as a companion, trying to convince passersby that it grew naturally against the open horizon. A lighthouse on the coasts of soy and corn.

For some reason, when I looked upon the single house, a chill rush of ice dripped from my elbows to my wrists. I could imagine a tornado ripping through its frame and blowing it across the surrounding fields. The clouds would gather over the treeless field in slow cycles while we all watched. The circling winds would pull to the earth, touch down in a fury of dirt and ripped apart crops; and tear through toward the house. I could see it. But, it could be a memory engraved into my Michigan-bred muscles.

But then again, my mind echoed the idea of the house splintering into pieces.

"There it is." Avery parked and the car shuttered. They made an arching wave with their hands. "Our place for tonight."

"Sick." I stepped out of the car first and tucked the newspaper under my arm. The pen found a place behind my ear and rested against the barrette I had shoved there after showering this morning—which, I had forgotten, needed to be taken out before it molded my hair to its bent shape. I slammed the door with one hand and unclipped the barrette in the other.

My notebook did not leave my hands, flipped to a new page in time with my first step. The pen behind my ear did not rest long. *Sense of dread. Rotted and chipped siding.* I scribbled with urgency, pacing on the lawn. *Overgrown and scratching grass. Depressing fields. Imagine ghosts in the window. Dead farmer? Killed investigators?*

Everyone followed with absent comments and the dull thudding of doors. Duffel bags hit the ground in a chorus of calls for extra help—but I didn't answer. My feet moved on their own, away from the car and toward the house. I had more impressions to write, I needed more to feed the jealous potential I had to perform. I could be better than the other reporter, I knew I could be; I could recall every chip of paint and stench of stale air. The reporter had not even been to the house.

Everything about it was eerie, yet I couldn't take my eyes away. Most people stare at morbid things, car accidents and the like, but I felt the same draw to the mundane. The brass doorknob shined against the weathered wood door, muting the porch around it. Sunset highlighted its shape, a rounded brass with a dip in the middle.

Beckoning in. Outstretched hand, fingers reaching. Swallowed inside. An ink spot pooled in the second W in 'swallowed'. My pen hovered.

What?

I didn't realize I had begun to walk toward the door until the toe of my shoe hit the first porch step. The broken wood made it impossible not to stumble and draw out creaking groans from the planks. Wind muffled the sound of clambering around the car.

That knob still shimmered.

The surface was as smooth as it looked, cool against my fingers and reflecting the lines in my palm. Though it made sense in its place, nestled in the aging entrance, I felt I had to convince myself it *did* belong there. Untarnished and unusual, wafting an air of welcome in opposition to the house it belonged to; strange and beautiful within my reach. When skin grasped metal, the wind calmed.

The breeze held me, caressing the back of my neck as a lover, and the intimidation of the house subsided into a mere echo. The door was unlocked, I could turn the brass without opposition. I twisted once but did not push; aided by the press of the air laying over my knuckles.

Words floated over the shell of my ear and collected at the edge of my mind, too far to grasp but enough to hint.

Open the door.

II.

We bought our first voice recorder at a garage sale a few summers ago. Fist full of five dollar bills, Avery argued the price down until the dented box was in our hands. It was sealed still, with its corners smashed as though it had been shoved away for years under mountains of useless things. Avery was the first to pull out their pocket knife and slice at the tape.

Recorders were little things. A small black rectangle donned with gray buttons and a green-tinted screen. Blake's hand snatched the box to draw out folded instructions while Avery and Hallie cooed over the plastic. We spent the night before researching what equipment we needed for an investigation while reruns of ghost-hunting dramas played through the static TV. I wrote them on a piece of notebook paper torn too quickly–a recorder, a camera. Computer. Flashlights. Tripod. Ouija board. A checklist, framed in frayed edges, to become the next famous crew.

Our first piece of equipment was in our hands, all that was left was to begin to test it. Blake explained how we would upload the files onto the computer and enhance them as the two friends did on TV—it was exciting. Avery had looked at me then, along with Hallie, both wearing grins that stretched to their ears.

"Isn't it exciting, Claire? Here, give it a try."

I felt something ripple down my throat. I could taste the words they said, in their bitter distaste, and swallow what Avery wanted. Always a show-off, but throwing me a bone. *I didn't try things first.* That was their selfish duty that became well-practiced. Hallie looked at me with her fluttering lashes and eager nods. Blake lifted his head to watch.

I took the plastic from Avery and looked over the buttons. One was bigger than the others and painted with a red circle. My thumb pressed it once until the screen blinked to life—REC. The others leaned in, holding their excited gushing behind their tongues while I couldn't think of a single word at all.

"...Hello."

I earned a few approving nods from Hallie.

"Hello, test. We are.... The Headless Ghostmen."

I shut off the recording and they all began to giggle. My smile broke as I gave the device to Blake and looked at Hallie. Hallie looked at Avery.

***

Blake dropped a duffel with a heavy grunt.

"So, how much cash is the reward? If we get evidence, I mean." The next fell with another *thump*, nearly drowning his voice. I pulled my hand back from the door to look, abandoning my effort to open the house. When my fingers left the brass, a spark left the surface like static—but it didn't pinch. Somehow, I felt guilty.

"Probably a load, they were falling apart in their last

interview." Avery joined with a laugh. The parents never disclosed an amount, from the papers and interviews we studied. From the begging and tears upon the mayor's podium, a few hundred seemed likely; at least, a decent reward for staying overnight, editing clips, and presenting a picture or two. They locked the car with a scraping *clunk* of their key. "Hundreds? A thousand, maybe? If we can prove a ghost killed them, we might be rich though."

Bitterness rose in my throat. A few hundred split into four was barely enough for anything.

If it was split only three ways, it would be more. Or, even one, it would be enough to support the editing fees for a book. There would be no need to work some meaningless job part-time, taking people's orders for pennies, or cleaning up after salary workers too good to throw out their own trash. The day could be spent writing, or drinking a coffee at a dimly lit cafe, while money did not line the edges of every thought.

"Well, let's go in!" Hallie declared with a pat on her knee, bouncing from her place behind the passenger door. It slammed decidedly and she was at Blake's side in seconds. Her elbow prodded at his arm. "I need to see this place, get a feel for the *danger*."

She winked at me over the car roof. Heat kindled in my cheeks.

She moved like an owl, her eyes level as they flickered back and forth to take in her surroundings. Her legs swung like the beat of wings with each step. Behind her irises, she held the knowledge of hundreds of books, theology and theory, hidden behind honey brown.

She joined me at the doorstep.

"I'll do the honors then, let's head in."

Not her. The whispered rumble of the wind returned, caressing the shell of my ear and filling it like smoke. I looked behind me to stare at the empty yard. Nothing but a distant rustle of dried leaves. Hallie reached forward to touch the knob in time with the smoke growing thicker, wet, clogging into a chorus of garbled depth–

Not her. Not her. Nothernothernothernothernothernothernothernothernot–

NOT HER HAND.

My arm lurched before I could think, slapping Hallie's wrist away and taking its place. The chaotic beating against my eardrum heightened to a static screech until my palm closed over brass and thrust forward.

The door opened and the screaming ceased.

Hallie stumbled with a harmony of wood creaking and hissed annoyance, "Claire, what the fuck..."

I didn't hear the rest. The rising tide of ringing in my ear centered in the now-open doorway, accumulating with the dust that drifted like snow onto the wood. The screaming voices didn't return, but it was as if they had left a burned imprint in the forefront of my mind, or released bees into my ear canal. The voice sounded unlike anyone I knew, inhuman maybe, and suffocating by speech alone.

Not her. I glanced at Hallie as she gestured to me with her lips pressed in a bitter line. *Not her?*

"Hey." A light shove pulled me from the ringing. Hallie pressed her fingers into my shoulder again, nails digging through the fabric. "Are you even listening? Not cool."

"I– sorry. Yeah." The words didn't feel like my own.

I fumbled over my thoughts, trying to think of an excuse. 'Sorry, I suddenly heard a million voices screaming in my ears. They made me do it?' Delusions could not account for shoving her back.

"What's going on up here?" Avery appeared behind Hallie, a bag in each hand and Blake trailing behind. In the light of the afternoon, a halo formed between the edges of their hair and the outline of the porch columns. "Hal flinched."

"Nothing."

"Yeah, nothing?" They quirked a brow. Blake stood on his toes to meet my gaze over Avery's shoulder. "You sure?"

I opened my mouth, reconsidered, and closed it. Hallie spoke before I could collect myself enough to try again, shrugging her shoulders and pressing past the rotting door frame. "Claire wanted first dibs in."

"Well, go ahead. Get your writing inspiration out now so you can help us with interviews later." Avery adjusted the handles in their palms, setting them on the porch to twist them and pick the straps up again. I watched their grip open to reveal the thin red lines underneath, swallowing back the realization that I did not have equipment in my hands.

I faced the open door. Lines burned into my skin– from clutching my notebook in stiff fingers until the paper edges cut against me. Three sets of eyes stared into my back. Not a single one moved. The hall revealed through the open door stretched before us in long floorboards and dark shadow, a tunnel abandoned in its time.

My hand found my pen again and wrote, lofted and without my eyes as guidance on the page. They were fixed on the open house waiting.

Split floorboards. Dusty rugs, stretching along the hall as runners. Furnished? Left without vandalism? They're watching me. Hung mirrors on the wall, maybe portraits. Eerie feelings, house breathing out intimidation.

I stepped forward and the floorboard creaked beneath my shoe. The others shuffled behind like ducklings following their mother, and let themselves be swallowed by the entry.

Cobwebs kissed my fingers as they rested against the wall, despite my attempts to avoid them. Dust breathed with me. One step to the side and invisible lace stuck to every part of me; face, neck– it didn't matter. I couldn't dodge them in the dim light of boarded windows and ratted curtains.

It feels like something is in here with us. Oddly quiet. You'll never get out.

Never get out? I paused, halfway between the living room's arch and the entry. The sunset through the door wafted in through dust streaks and waved from the fields. I could imagine it like a horror movie, where the door slammed shut behind us and we wail with fear– the locks clicking and refusing to let us out, shadows seeping from the walls to grab at us with cold fingers and drag us screaming into the cellar–

"In here?" Blake began to pile bags in the living room; a square space complete with an untouched fireplace and molding couches. His voice drew me into the room again, letting my notebook fall to the side and rest against my jeans. When Blake dropped another bag down, plumes rose along a round rug but did not give a clearer view of what pattern hid underneath.

Past the fireplace, a dining room opened through another arch. Two chairs were missing from the table set– or what I assumed to be a set of four. The curtains were drawn there too, and behind the table stood a door half ripped from the hinges.

Kitchen. All these old houses had a similar layout— my hometown was familiar with the farmhouses that popped up like sprouts as people settled in. The living room and dining room, a connected kitchen, bathroom downstairs— bedrooms above and cellar below. This layout accounted for a kitchen closed by a door— off its hinges but still painted with a grimy jade and what I assumed to be white. It clung pathetically to the frame in a limp 'V' between its side and the dark frame.

I stared into the wood, at nothing at all. Something ripped it from the hinges. *A hand had come round the panel and torn, maybe from rage– or blew it from the frame in a burst of ghostly energy–*

The inspired words were coming easier than they ever had.

In the dining room, steps creaked until Avery's grin appeared. I hadn't noticed they had left.

"Alright! Briefing!" They clapped once in finality, a practice they used to introduce every investigation. I never cared much for briefing before the mission. It ruined the authenticity of exploring a place with fresh, unbiased eyes. I would have rather toured the house alone, *then* come together.

But I wasn't our "leader".

Avery passed me with an inflated chest and no excuse when their hip bumped mine. Hallie followed, lingering at my side a moment to draw her hand across the base of my spine once. "Excuse me."

Forgiven from the front door.

"I scoped out the first floor, and I really want to start,"

Avery began, "I think I'll start down here in the kitchen with Hal. Blake, how do you feel about set-up time?"

"Twenty minutes, maybe?" Blake twisted a camcorder onto a tripod, brows furrowed in concentration. The screen lit up when he opened the side, and then promptly shut off again. "The upstairs cameras are ready."

"We'll take motion sensor light and do a quick scope for clues. When that's done, we'll come to help you get stuff set up here for a base. Claire, can you take the cameras upstairs?"

"Yeah, I can." I took the two tripods from Blake, tucking them into my arm. My notebook bent under the metal legs– but I couldn't adjust it. "Bedrooms?"

"Bathroom and hallway," Avery suggested, "then we'll come back again and decide who's going where once it gets dark. We'll send Blake up with you after."

"How creepy is it?" Blake's face twisted while he wrung at a flashlight in his hands. "Did you see any blood? Where they, y'know– died?"

"There wasn't any, remember? No physical evidence, they need the spooky stuff—that's our job."

"Right, right. Proof of any kind." Blake mumbled.

The hardwood under my feet gave an awkward groan as I ventured closer. The article mentioned the master bedroom as an interest in the past, but a reason was never listed. "Why the bathroom?"

Mirror. The answer sighed from the walls. I looked over the wallpaper, the fireplace, the faces of my team– and nothing changed.

"Not sure, honestly. A hunch." Avery shrugged, "seemed kinda off. Let's get going, we'll start down here."

"Set it up nice!" Hallie laughed as Avery linked their arms. She plucked the device in Blake's hand and waved it. "I want to know what we're dealing with. Get me a good shot, okay? We can do an EVP together later."

"C'mon, duck." Avery tugged her toward the kitchen, earning a squealing laugh in return. They deserted the room within seconds. I could still hear them giggling beyond the wall.

I glared too harshly at the wallpaper.

"Do you, like... want me to come with you upstairs?" Blake blinked up at me from his place among wires and black canvas. He had begun to lay out equipment on an old beach towel. The cartoon faces had long since faded, I remember stealing it from the back of my bathroom cupboard. No matter how hard we shook it, it somehow still had sand nestled in the fibers from lake trips nearly twenty years before. Blake set a plastic recorder over what used to be an eye. I bent to pocket it.

"Why? This place creeps you out that much? You'd be alone down here if I go."

He shifted in place and turned his attention to the last of the gadgets. His voice wavered, despite speaking a single word. "Yeah."

A few moments passed between us.

"Stay here, don't let Avery bully you into leaving the room if you don't want to." The wrinkles in Blake's forehead relaxed when he nodded. "I mean it. Focus on stuff down here with the lanterns on."

"Thanks."

"Sure." I made my way to the door, pulling the knobs to

close them with me. "I'll be back down. If you see the others before me–tell them I'm exploring for our account."

"I will. Be careful."

III.

It started as a race. Blake proposed it, socks upon newly polished wood until one of us reached the second floor. It took a single misstep against the wax surface to send my body back, flailing, under the watch of hung picture frames and beige walls. No matter how many times I tried to recall that moment, I could not remember if it lasted a second or an hour-- but the feeling of my arm pinned beneath my back and the single crack ending the fall never escaped my memory.

He won. I lost.

My parents left us alone that night. They weren't there to witness Blake, wide-eyed and panting from victory, staring down at my body. He did not move, but neither did I. I laid there, without tears, pinned between my own spine and the hardwood. The lamp next to Blake extended the shadows beneath the open gape of his mouth and collected in the dips of his cheeks. They danced there, in the muscles that tensed and relaxed, scrambling his features akin to what I imagined a biblical angel to be. Dark, unknown, and overshadowed with light.

***

The stairs I walked, sandwiched as an afterthought between

two walls, were less of a divine image. Nothing remotely holy awaited me at the top of the staircase. Even when I squinted, the outlines upstairs were blurred.

Beneath my feet, the steps cracked in patterns that reminded me of worn leather—their paint was discolored and chipped from each splinter. I planted my hand against the wallpaper and bent at the waist, assessing the true depth of the rot. Visiting old houses was a bonus to our ghostly adventures. The detail kept secrets, like value and outdated trends, that always served as the greatest inspiration. Any inspiration, even if fleeting in old wood, was worth a second glance.

Find me in the closet.

From the step's surface, a mouth began to split from the cracks. It widened with a gaping grin, pulling back the grains to smile splinters up at me. I yanked away, my eyes darting to the next step up. I was imagining things, the shadows were collecting in the corners of my vision– that explained why the lines in the wood were morphing into murmurs and whispering to me. I imagined it.

Find me.

"What–" I flinched, planting my hand on the wallpaper. Beneath my palm, the dry paper thrummed, seeping with the voice in my mind. Again, it pestered like an itch against the wrong side of my eardrum.

Find me.

Where my hand rested, the paper boiled in the same morphing way as the wood– dizzying and unclear. Between the bubbling beneath my feet and the blistering wall, the air tightened.

I was imagining things. I *must* have been imagining things.

The voice cooed from the inside of my ear, intruding from inside, not the wall– the walls could not speak. The floor could not melt beneath me. The staircase was not narrowing. *There was no creature, climbing up two steps after me, long fingers reaching for my ankles.*

My heart deafened my hearing with loud pulses. I could barely make out the distinctive creak of the wood as I began to ascend once more. One step. Two– I could not look behind me. I could see it there, scraping against the steps and snapping its skewed jaws like a wild dog. *Getting faster. Reaching for my ankle.*

Something cold brushed my skin.

I sprinted to the second floor. With each thwack of my heels hitting wood, there was an image of the creature scrambling in time. I could see it when I shut my eyes, flailing and getting close enough to bite out a searing chunk of my skin, snapping with each thought and heartbeat.

I could see it, imprinted into the backs of my eyelids as I blindly ascended. *A dark entity rising from the landing and crawling behind me, on all fours and jaw open to show a beastly set of fangs. Its head would crack and pop as it rotated upside down. Its red eyes would stare unblinking at me as they widened without eyelids. It would chase me with broken, mangled limbs at an ungodly speed and rattle out long breaths, groans, and clicks as it grew closer. It would gain ground on me, catching my ankle in its claws and yanking down, its face screeching and etching permanently into my mind–*

My steps landed with a defined stomp against the wood and my head turned to whatever was chasing.

Nothing.

***

Silence greeted me in the bedroom. It held as much dust as the hall before it, lining the bedposts and window, down to the weathered nightstand and fading carpet. Cobwebs, again, curtained every visible square of the ceiling– until it was a muddy mix of dirty beige and gray.

I made quick work of balancing the camcorder on the tripod, shoving it into a corner to capture the majority of the room. Before I left, I would remember to pose it in the doorway– the mental note from the last investigation returned to the forefront of my mind. Blake had complained for hours about having a bad shot in the last house's bedroom. Avery had reminded me twice to remember it this time.

My jaw tightened with the screw I turned.

The best piece of evidence we had ever captured was an orb. It had been on a camera that Blake was too scared to set up, forcing me to venture alone into the brewery's basement to place it myself. I remember feeling a chill crawl over my shoulder when I left the room, and sure enough, checking the footage revealed a little white orb flung into my sweatshirt.

We celebrated with pizza that night, from the *second* cheapest option in town. Slices in hand, we replayed the video over and over again, zooming in, enhancing, and submitting it to online blogs– it was a rush of *purpose*. Worth. We had gathered something.

The blog rejected my article. Hallie held my shoulder when I told her, a fresh sheen of tears over my eyes, and told me to try again next time. Then again, the next time. And again, the investigation after.

This was the last one. Our final attempt. If the evidence

was good and my article had material, I could finally stop that unemployed dead end from creeping closer. I could have a writing job. I could be sponsored on a blog. I would be famous for what I loved to do.

This needed to work.

Once comforted by the blinking red light beneath the camcorder's lens, I stepped away. One camera down. Our usual routine was a camera set up, individual investigation, meeting, then partners– it worked well enough. Blake was the only one who stayed in one place, huddled among our equipment and battery lanterns.

Open the closet.

The voice itched at me again. Low, dripping from the walls– I stepped closer to the wallpaper to stare at the staggered print of flowers and fake ribbon. The style was one I remembered from my grandmother's house. I scratched at the faded petals, testing how much would come off with a mere scrape of my nail. The moon outside the window shifted. My hand blended with the darkness of the wall.

My nail buried into something soft, like plaster still wet.

Moving.

Breathing.

I yanked my hand back to dislodge my finger from the wallpaper, disgust building in my throat. Acid turned in my stomach as the shadows pulsed at my touch. The stair creature returned to my mind. *If I was facing the wall, fighting with nothing to release my hand, what was stopping it from crawling around the door behind me? I could imagine its legs, breaking and stepping over each other while they scrambled forward as an insect. Its head turned in a perpetual tilt upside down and jaw unhinged, a soundless screech–*

My finger freed.

I spun, half expecting the stair creature to be lurching at me from the hallway, and flinched.

Nothing, again. The hall was dark but nothing stood out of place. It felt as unsettling as every other haunted location the team had been to, though I never had imagined creatures rabidly chasing me throughout the investigation.

Two steps. I managed to take two steps toward the door before it slammed in a loud *bang*.

Perhaps this was how the two died. Chased and torn apart by uneven fangs and ripping claws, not of this world and leaving no mark– if it killed me too, at least the others would have it on tape–

The closet.

Two single, white-paneled doors stood beside me. Though the layer of paint was sloppily painted over long ago and chipping, I could make out the outline of two button knobs. My palm fell against one, giving an experimental tug, and the doors parted.

A hand mirror lay alone on the floor, in a thin circle of dust.

Look.

I did not want to look. I would stare at the entire world, taking in every sight– except what reflection awaited me. Yet, with shaking hands and a sweating palm, I gripped the handle and brought it level with my face.

I saw my own eyes first, wide. Brown.

And a set of blue behind me.

IV.

Our first overnight exploration took place in a house. A friend from elementary school with an affinity for ghost-hunting television shows ran into Blake in a grocery aisle and offered her mother's empty rental property– and before we could refuse, a key was pressed into Avery's palm.

I tried not to get in the way of Blake's cameras– two, the first time– as he set them up on tripods pointing into rooms. Nor did I bother Avery as they gleefully unpacked every duffel we brought and lined their contents up on the dining room table. We were given permission to stay the night, and Avery insisted on keeping our belongings all in one room. *Base camp*, they called it. Like what they had seen in the famous investigations. My notebook and pen felt minuscule in importance, compared to their carefully drafted itinerary.

"Claire, Blake is still nervous. I'll take him with me and we'll take the recorder to the basement. Can you and Hal take the upstairs?"

A flush crawled on the underside of my skin, spanning over my neck and jaw in heated pinpricks. Hallie answered for us. "Sure, sure. We'll go upstairs."

I turned to her after Avery fumbled for a moment.

Satisfaction painted itself into her face with a smirk, dotted into quick an uptick on her cheeks. They had been arguing leading up to the investigation, competing with each other on the order things would be done. *Who decides what to do or when they should do them. Funding for the overnight stay. What would happen after.* Their arguments always grew the same; from a bud of annoyance into a loud, blossomed flower. And by the hurt measured in Avery's face, this had overgrown. They didn't answer. I preferred it that way. I'd side with Hallie with anything. *Everything*, if she asked. I had no protest to her hand in mine, parting us from the others and ascending upstairs.

The doorway scraped my shoulder as she pulled me into the room, fingers hooked and tugging my shirt until we were both behind the bedroom door. With a kick of her foot, she closed the door and it clicked, leaving us to shakily breathe against the darkness.

The air was stale. With every inhale came dust, and with the dust came the gentle scent of lavender perfume. When Hallie moved her hair from her shoulder it grew stronger, wafting and licking at my cheeks in hot plumes. I could smell it on her neck too, as she boxed me against the wall between her forearms and leaned in.

"Claire," Hallie whispered, "I turned off the camera in here."

Against the far wall, moonlight fell against the fly corpses upon the windowsill. It let just enough light in—enough to glint off the swing of Hallie's pendant, to outline a halo of frizz in her hair, to catch on the outline of her shoulders as they dropped. Her face was shadowed by the empty house, but it made her no less beautiful.

I felt my heart seize in my chest. It beat against the wall pressed into my back in a steady thrum of flustered bewilderment.

"You did?" I whispered back, though my words were filled with less fluidity than hers. Mine cracked on the second syllable.

"Uh-huh." She hummed and took a step closer. "I wanted a second alone."

"What about Avery?" Cursed to haunt my mind. I didn't want to think of them, in their suave grip they had on Hallie. They were still doing a solo recording in the basement, there was no way they could hear—and if the camera was off, the recordings wouldn't go through—

"They aren't here. It's us." Hallie let a hand rest along the waistband of my jeans, hooking her thumb in the belt loop. Her other hand stayed planted on the wall. "Do you…"

She didn't continue. I could hear my heartbeat in my ears. Her shirt brushed the tips of them from its extension to the wallpaper. I could not manage more than a whisper. "Do I what?"

Hallie leaned in, sharing a breath between our lips as she lowered her voice to match my own shaking murmur. Her head tilted down for a moment to watch her own thumb stroke along the denim she held. As if counting stitches there, she paused.

"Do you *like* me, Claire?" Her head tilted upward, eyes meeting mine. I could feel her thumb slide over the ridge of my jeans and tuck along the underside of my waist.

I felt her kiss on my lips for a week after.

***

I wished to throw the mirror across the closet and stamp the surface into shards, but my muscles froze in place. I could not bend my elbows, nor turn my head to see the full image of the woman staring at me behind my shoulder. I could only sputter out heaving breaths and try to avoid death by shock in the middle of the bedroom.

I had seen the woman's face before— I memorized that face. Printed in ink, below headlines, on screen, and now staring back at me.

Dread enclosed as an ice sheet over me. My legs would not move.

The woman's reflection did not move, either. *She would lurch from behind as I watched helpless, long nails digging into my collar until the skin burst beneath them, strangle me, rip me with an unhinged jaw or swallow my limbs into the walls. I will be next, my face would be on a newspaper. Unhinged. Feral. Leaping from behind.*

I blinked. She remained.

You came here to investigate. Again, the voice spoke from inside my ears. It was neither masculine nor feminine, and the reflection did not move her lips. She stayed, unblinking and staring into my own. I could imagine them warping in ripples of sound, speaking through a ghoul facade, and reaching my mind. Her mouth would melt into the dark, but her statements would hang between us. *I know why.*

"I–" My vocal cords were freed from the grasp she held on them, air rushing back into my lungs in a fury of dust. A cough protested against my rushed excuse, "we'll leave! Now, we'll leave right now!"

She would know my claim was a film over the true reason we came. The group wouldn't leave, not if I said we needed to— they would stay. We needed this, no matter the risk. I needed this, no matter the risk.

I feared blinking. She could lunge, sink her nails into me— or burst through the mirror glass and thrash at my throat. My eyes watered while they wondered how that void mouth would open, what words would pour from ink—

I know what you came for.

V.

I scowled at the slow drip of diet soda over my thumb. The styrofoam cup I clenched did nothing to absorb the sticky tear, and no matter how many times I tried to rub the residue off my finger, all I accomplished was a smeared stain over the diner's green-lined logo.

Green, in various shades, dominated the dining room. Limp wilted salad in an untouched salad bar. The scratched font above a burger line, advertising the "best burger in town"— in a town with very few restaurants at all. A water-damaged lime backdrop for an unchanged "quote of the week" printed on a sheet of paper– *Jesus Loves You!*

Alternating maroon and olive choral rows of squeaking booths, cracked where spines pressed. All were empty, save for the second to last by the window. I approached the trio's overlapping conversation with my tray in hand, setting it down with a loud clack while I slipped next to Blake's side. He had a straw wrapper in his hands and was fiddling with it somehow; folding it over itself back and forth with a quiet smile.

"Took you forever, huh? How hard is it to make burgers?" Hallie laughed, popping three fries in her mouth at once. Avery greeted me with a shrug.

"Hal, you've never worked in a kitchen." They didn't bother looking over. Their hands were closed on a chili dog, slathered in condiments, and squeezed between their fingers. Against the paneled wood wall and framed fish, their studded jacket stood out of place. "You've got no authority on line cooks."

"But still." Hallie pouted. "I've made them at home."

"Nope, still none."

"Because you're the expert, obviously." Blake quipped with a roll of his eyes. His tray of fries– the smallest, he had asked for but did not seem to receive– was halfway finished. He hadn't been eating much since our debut success.

We were moving up in the world. Worth celebration, even, in the form of plastic cafeteria trays and a two-for-one burger night. The evidence of our last investigation was edited and submitted alongside my article to a popular online archive an hour before we parked in the near-empty parking lot. It would take a day or two to hear back. Our last investigation proved fruitful– I glanced at Hallie over the beaded lip of my drink. She finished her fries and began on Avery's.

Two men came to sit three tables over, a man and his son. Their baseball caps and faded t-shirts foreshadowed their extensive conversation about fishing and college sports.

"Sure, I am." They flashed a grin at their food. "It's a shame a cooking show hasn't called me up."

The line earned a chuckle from Hallie. Blake didn't bother looking up from his strewn fry basket. After a few moments of quiet chewing and eavesdropping over what team had won last Friday, Avery spoke before I could.

"What's up, Blake?"

His head shook in protest when he was addressed, but the movement must have caught in his throat; he coughed into his jacket sleeve.

"No, seriously," Avery leaned on their elbows across their half-eaten plate. If I was not directly next to the pair, I wouldn't have been able to hear how their voice dipped. "You've been quieter than usual."

"I'm fine."

"You're picking at fries and look like you're about to puke. Are you sick?" The question was spoken a bit louder than the sentence before it. Hallie leaned in to hear the answer, I kept my head tilted toward the wooden panel wall behind her head. Blake did not like eyes on him. I respected it.

"I'm–" I felt the sleeve of his jacket tug against mine. "—Fine. I'm fine."

Hallie was next to inquire with a careful lean, tucking her hair behind her ear so there was no chance of dipping a curl in ketchup. "Did the investigation make you that upset? I know you felt that hand on your back but–"

" – Hal, maybe it's better to leave the details out."

"Right, right. Sorry." Hallie nodded after Avery's interruption. I picked up my cup and took a drink.

"I think," Blake cautiously started, "I don't want to go anymore."

In the next two investigations, he did not.

***

My palms pressed into the floor. Like a curling smoke behind my ears, the presence of a dead woman crawled and filled my head with intoxication. I could feel her fingers sliding along the underside of my cheeks from the back of my neck, splayed wide beneath my hair– slipping against my skin and morphing to the shape of my bones. *What if they melted there? If they fused into my skin and laced into my neck until we were a throbbing picture of grotesque monstrosity, would we pulse as the walls did? Could she swallow me whole? Would I witness her reflection break and snap, unhinge as the maw of a snake and reveal a void behind sharp teeth? Would I feel them, when they sank into my neck and tore at the stringed tendons?* Fear prickled beneath the non-existent pads of her fingertips.

What do you want the most?

My jaw tightened. At that moment, I wished for nothing greater than to tear my stare from the mirror–from the stare that stood unmoving behind me. They weren't as I expected eyes to be. Instead of familiar warmth and emotion, a cool indifference reflected to my own."To– to be successful. For once, to be successful."

I did not intend to speak. The words were pulled out on a fishing line and hung for her, right along the mirror's edge. My mouth was wet with saliva and I swallowed back the urge to vomit. When my esophagus contracted, I felt a thin hair scratch down the length of my throat.

What is success?

"I..." The question clutched my voice. Lying to a ghost, when she had just drawn my answer from the depths of my gut. I could imagine her doing the same again, reaching in with those cold fingers and scaping the truth from me. My words rushed from me in a hoarse whisper. Shame clawed at my tongue. "My work– I don't want a stupid, passive life. I want to be famous."

Famous. The word vibrated against my eardrums. *Famous.*

Famous. Famous. I wanted to be well-known. I wanted to be validated. To be recognized as worth something, for the things I have done— or the things I could do. Was that famous?

I would do anything to be more than I was.

Anything.

I swallowed again, around the thin hair that lodged itself against the back of my tongue and gagged. My eyes watered, blurred— and I brought a hand up to wipe at them. The cuff of my sleeve tugged at the corner of my eyelid.

It would rip. It would tear my skin with a single tug and separate my lashes, it would split above the socket. The cold fingers caressing my ear would reach around and dig their ghostly nails between fissures and tug it farther—

I stood, dropping the mirror.

Get out. The command surrounded me, internally and externally, in an omnipresent wave of order. Leave. *Leave.* My knees groaned as they stretched with each of my panicked strides to the door. I tried the knob. Nothing. No turn, no click of a lock, no movement.

"Let me out!" I meant to yell, but just a whisper made it past my lips. Hoarse. Tied by that snaking, damned hair. "Let me *out—*"

Underneath my palm, the metal licked and burned. I yanked my hand away and cradled it to my chest. The room remained empty of apparitions and beasts, but the walls twisted in their peeling paper and scuffed baseboard. *Warping. Shrinking. Gaping. Swimming.*

In the corner of my eye, a shadow along the floor flailed and snapped its jaws.

It took four haphazard strides to reach the window. Dust

coated my fingertips while they tugged fruitlessly at the lip of the windowpane, and again when they fumbled with the metal latch. Fly corpses puffed from my frantic attempts and fell like snow across my feet.

Trapped. I was trapped. I couldn't get out, I couldn't leave—

The others.

If the others died, escape would be possible. If they died, I would escape. Right?

My breath escaped me, beyond what I could hope to catch. I was better than dying here, I had more to offer— if they died here, they would be another story in the paper, or immortalized in a book. I froze.

Better than them.

A twinge pinched in my chest. The words, faint as a breeze yet circling in tandem within my ears, held me suspended. *Was that all I wished to hear? How I was better than the company I kept?* A selfish, prickling part of me clawed at the statement with greedy hands- I was better. I wanted to believe so.

I spent months writing. Editing. Listening to Avery's self-serving praise of doing the bare minimum and waiting for applause. Watching Blake and Hallie excel at skills they loved, while all my tangible proof failed me into the cold font of a rejection email. *Had I been waiting to hear the praise?*

I liked it. Despite morality and justification – I *liked* it.

I wanted more.

I believe in you.

If the house wanted a sacrifice, wanted to trap people within its walls— it would not be me. I would be sure of it,

I would be successful. Worth something more than them, at last, I would be the one praised. The payment would be made, and delivered by me if that was what it took.

My eyes came back to the mirror. The rush of shadow and movement from the walls had ceased. The only sound in my ears was the slow creak of my steps to where the gilded frame lay, and my knees knocking in a soft rap against the floor. The second face had dissipated at some point, leaving the peeling wall and shadow behind the crest of my ear. Yet, with no apparition over my shoulder, I still felt the linger of her presence. I could see her, crawling along the lines of my neck and hovering over the crown of my hair. My attention continued to the rounded curve of my cheekbone, where it sloped into my jaw– my jaw. My mouth moved in a lip-tilted, half-whisper.

I met my own, unblinking stare. I wasn't feeling my mouth move, but the reflection continued as if it had recorded me saying the words in glee.

I believe in you.

I believe in you.

I believe in you.

VI.

"I think I want to go to school." Blake pulled at his plastic straw with a sharp screech, never taking his gaze off the remaining drops of scarlet fruit punch clinging to his drink lid. He made the melody a few more times. Up and down, refusing silence. "I'm not totally sure, but I was looking. For a while, I guess, I've been looking."

Squeak.

"What? When?" I readjusted in the backseat so my shoulders were perpendicular to his. One pressed into the soft upholstery- the other was tense to avoid dropping my own paper cup. My feet crumpled the paper fast food bag we had designated for trash and tucked it on the floor. *Squeak.* I looked for the answer, expected an answer in the form of some admission; but Blake simply shrugged and pinched his straw again. "For what?"

"Computers? Tech stuff." *Squeak.* "IT or programming. There's a certificate program an hour away."

The last sentence was said in a suspension of his instrument's sounds. Instead of continuing, he chewed at his bottom lip.

"But– what? When do you want this? Are you moving?"

I moved my seat belt behind my head to free my torso, leaning closer. His expression muddied with guilt, shame maybe, but I found studying it hard. My heart fell into the cradle of my last rib.

He was planning to leave.

"Blake," I started again, "I don't get it– how are you going to pay fo–"

"— It's a work-study." He finished the question before it could fully escape me. "It pays. Enough to stay in a shared apartment. I found it all online, it starts in August."

August. Blake would leave for school in August. I would still be here, with no steady job, with no qualifications– he had agreed with me, they were overrated. *We spent at least one night a month ranting about how much of a scam post-secondary was, we made fun of–*

"Hallie and Avery helped me sign up."

My back hit the seat cushion with an audible thump. The pair were out of the car and currently picking out pints of discounted ice cream at our local grocery. Blake and I usually stayed in the parking lot on these occasions– but after the confession, I wished I had volunteered to go in instead.

"Of course they did," I muttered to the driver's headrest. They both did school. Hallie graduated. Avery attended community college every other night. Blake and I didn't bother– but now, only *I* didn't. Anger licked up my fingers. I clenched them. "So you're just gonna leave?"

"I'll do the last investigation, I think." Blake's voice muffled as he replaced his lip with the drink's straw. "After missing the last few... I think I'll go one more time."

I watched Hallie and Avery exit the automatic door,

crowded together in the single door frame and laughing while they squeezed through. Avery held the bag. Hallie kept fighting to take it. I wanted to scream, to argue- to accuse them and Blake of betrayal, spite, and contempt- but I sat in silence, wondering if my seething and clenched teeth would psychically break the car window.

"I'm sorry, Claire. I'll come to visit a lot." Blake pleaded next to me. I didn't look at him but gave my answer in a flat tone.

"I'm glad you're coming with us, at least."

***

I could barely feel the wood beneath the slick of my palm as it stuttered against the banister. Each slap against the splintered wood grain solidified the plan— *continue the investigation. Finish the investigation.*

Get what is deserved.

The snapping shadows that plagued my ascent allowed me down. The wallpaper did not waver, did not melt and shift and squeeze under the brush of my skin— there was no creeping image of fear waiting to lunge. It fell away to the silent deal and sound of my soles upon creaking stairs.

A small laugh echoed at the landing. I paused.

I would be the only one out. *I had to be, or we would all be trapped. I would be trapped.* That would make the difference in this investigation and the last investigation within these walls. This one would succeed with a survivor.

I passed into the parlor and a hand clapped my shoulder.

"Claire!" Avery greeted with a grin, "We're about to set up for our recordings."

Blake and Hallie were squatting next to his laptop, the

former fumbling with a cord of some kind until the recorder popped free. He handed it to her and then moved to grab another. We had three, in preparation to do this investigation, and considered it a necessary investment.

"So, I'm thinking," Avery began as they retreated back to the pair, "we'll—"

"—I want to go together," I interrupted. Avery's brow furrowed when they looked to me. We never went together and had never gotten along well enough to attempt it, but we *needed* to. My heart skipped and my gut clenched— *we needed to be alone*. "I want to record with two people in the basement, I'll go with you. While Blake and Hallie do their stuff on the main floor."

"Why?" Hallie chimed, confusion also muddying her expression. "You two? Would you rather me go?"

"No, no, I," *an excuse*. I needed an excuse. "I'll take a camcorder, and Avery can do something solo. I want to record, and I think it might be too much for Blake to do in the basement. You should see the upstairs, Hallie, there's this dust circle that looks— uh... religious."

Her eyes lit up. Blake's did too, out of gratefulness.

"Oh, sure. That works, then." Avery coughed out the approval with a nod of their head, reaching for a recorder. They rolled it in their palm, focusing on the action rather than my own. Blake offered a camcorder and mouthed a 'thanks'.

"Alright, cool. Good luck guys." Hallie waved us off, her bright smile a beacon among the dust and forgotten grime. She would rival the sun. I felt a pang in my chest. I would remember her as such. Glittering, and unfortunate. "We'll meet back in an hour? Do uploads and have snacks before doing some lock-ins?"

"Sounds good, have fun, Hal," Avery called over their shoulder and led us forward, past the threshold of the kitchen arch.

I watched them, stepping in their footfalls. The basement door waited for us on rusted hinges, painted a faded vermilion and speckled with remains of white. It squeaked when Avery pulled it ajar.

Darkness loomed before them. *From behind their head, it crawled and beckoned— like hands, outstretched and reaching to dig into the cotton of their shirt and yank them down into the abyss. Would I stop it? Or would I watch feral shadows rip at them with every inch they sunk into the house's cellar?*

They paused. Then, they pressed the recorder's power button.

Avery descended first. I glanced around the kitchen, along the broken cabinet doors and cracked counters until — *there*. I let out a breath. A knife block laid on its side, with two handles lodged in its slits. I called out to Avery, and their sinking red light— REC. "Go on, I'll follow."

I held my breath, afraid to hear the sound of it shaking. *This was what needed to be done.* This or trapped. *This or trapped*. I was doing as I needed.

It would be easy.

My hand locked around the bigger of the two hilts, and pulled. A knife left the block with a scrape. Still sharp. My heartbeat sped. I turned it over once in my palm, staring at my savior.

Hands joined mine, invisible touch cupping the top of my

knuckles to close them around the handle. She was behind me, her head next to my shoulder and breathing along my ear.

It would be easy.

Go.

I walked with her over my shoulder, hand over my hand in holding the weapon. The open doorway awaited me, and I lingered there, fixed upon the little red light bouncing softly with Avery's descent. It blinked. *Again.* The knife in my hand stayed heavy.

I stepped down once and reached behind me to close the door with a *click.*

***

"Is there anyone in the room with us right now?"

"My name is Avery, and this is Claire, could you say our names or let us know you're he— hey, Claire, you okay?"

Shuffling. A single crack of static.

"Claire? Hey— Claire!"

The loud, muffled rumblings of being dropped onto cement and skidding away.

A single, interrupted scream. The dull pounding of a knife into flesh.

REC - END.

VII.

Eleven investigations. I helped them with eleven investigations. Eleven summaries were written, submitted, and documented. I kept them all.

***

Knives lodged too easily in a person's chest. My bicep strained while it tugged the blade free from Avery's lifeless body, forcing it to rip from the flesh and blood it had punctured.

It was done. One was done.

The red light of the recorder blinked behind Avery's head, scraped and forgotten on the ground. I moved from my straddle of their torso, lifting my leg from the pooling scarlet puddle and pushing forward on my palm to press the button off.

I debated smashing it, ruining the black plastic until it was a mangled twist of wire intestines. Eliminate my evidence—*was it evidence?* It was condemning, it was the wrong idea. I did this to save myself. *Self-defense. To get out.*

It wouldn't help my story. My fame. My escape. My narrative.

I raised the box in my trembling hand and brought it

down onto the concrete. Once. My strength had betrayed me, pathetic and floundering over the action like I was in the thick fog of a dream. The recorder bounced on the floor with a chipped click. I frowned. My chest swelled with an emotion I did not recognize, burning, like anger, but filling my lungs past any rage I felt before. I brought the box down again, harder.

It didn't break. *Why wouldn't it break?* The sticking feeling bubbled in the bottom of my lungs and I flung the plastic at the ground again. The third time, it cracked where the red light blinked. *That bright eye wouldn't watch me, hear me anymore— there would be no history to misunderstand. The only eyes that would watch were those witnessing the conditions to my escape, the ones that lodged themselves in the dark, in the mortar of cement blocks, and under the planks of the stairs.*

My shoulders heaved.

It was done. I killed Avery.

Was she watching me? From the spider-infested stairs? Did she sit on the dust and rest her chin in her dead hands, grinning in a split smile at my obedience to the house's offer? If I looked, I would see her get up to greet me. She would descend to me, take me in her cold fingers again and her face would warp like a flame—unclear, except for the focal center of a beady black void.

Underneath my knees, blood crawled into the fiber of my jeans. I stood.

I expected the knife to outweigh the confusion in my head. I expected regret and remorse to pour from where blood dripped, but it didn't come—nothing did.

"I didn't want to," I spoke aloud, but to whom, I couldn't

place. To the house, maybe. To myself, to convince myself of my reluctance, to make it a harder decision the next two times.

A shaking inhale. *The others.*

Avery would have been easiest. We weren't close. We had an understanding with each other of mutual apathy, that we would never try to be friendly outside of our circle— they took Hallie's attention and Blake's reverence. They were proud. Arrogant. Justification steadied my hands when they plunged.

With the others... the knife did not feel right. Knives were angry and violent, the method of revenge and frustration pent too long—they did not deserve the same. But they had to go. They needed something else. Forgiving, regretful; even when it took their life.

My hand kept the knife gripped as I started towards the stairs, holding a hand out in the darkness to find guidance. A single, murky window offered moonlight along the far wall of the room, tucked behind a half wall and casting a filtered glow over unfinished floors. Avery's body lay on that side, with just enough light to illuminate the spreading puddles that cradled them. *Seeping. Would it reach the cobwebs along the floor? The wet walls? The mildewed cracks of the root cellar door, on the opposite side?*

How far would it spread?

I swallowed and felt for the rough surface of the wall. Sticking cobwebs wound along my fingers as I began to round the corner of the little room to face the utter darkness of the main chamber— the basement door squeaked atop the stairs. Light slivered into the room.

"Avery? Claire?"

No. Oh, no, no, no— Hallie's voice called from the ground floor. She wasn't supposed to come down. I would do something differently, something merciful and fitting for *her*. She wouldn't end as a mess on the floor like Avery deserved, s*he—*

The knife was in my hand.

Heavy boot soles pressed on the stairs. One by one, they creaked with her shifting weight. *Did she hold the metal rail? Was she worried the boards would snap beneath her? That the dip in the wood grain was enough to break under her, sudden and quick into concrete, the grace of something higher to save me from doing it myself?*

Step. Another. Another. A click. Light washed the steps in a narrow cone. I retreated behind the joining room again. *Back with Avery.*

"Guys— say something, it's freaking me out."

Her voice vibrated against my rib cage. The flashlight bounced with her descent and I counted the steps it would take for her to reach the floor. To see the blood. The knife in my hand. Her end.

Four. Light rushed over the floor. A long crack ran along the center, breaking into a delta over a metal drain. Sweat built beneath my palm.

Three. I wiped my hand on my jeans, but it didn't dry. It wouldn't dry. I passed the knife back and forth, trying to imagine how I could do this with swiftness.

Two. She would watch me. The walls, the house— they would watch me. I would prove I could escape, that I was better than them, that I was worthy of the wish she promised to grant.

One.

I did not speak. I did not remember moving. The flashlight's metal casing skittered across the floor and rolled past fate awaiting until it stopped at my feet.

VIII.

I watched myself from the walls. I do not know when they swallowed my body and bound me to their mortar, nor when they forged me into a piece of their immovable face. Their stones pierced the cotton of my shirt back, dug into me— in wet cobwebs I had traced before. I would soon fuse with them entirely. I would spread my arms and feel moist rock let me in, soak me in, to the house that claimed my mind.

The knife killed Hallie. I did not feel the same rage pulse through me, somehow— from here, as my audience, I felt nothing at all. I watched a film, starring my movement. A kill. A grip on a knife. Movements, stiff and reluctant, in the dim cone of the flashlight.

Did I feel anything? Did I feel sorry? Regretful?

The pendant of Hallie's necklace tangled in her hair where she lay. My hand plucked it out of her curls and laid it back against her collar.

My body walked to the staircase, out of the humble light left spilled. It glittered warm against the scarlet pools and speckled floor behind my back. In the space between two bodies, that recorder blinked red.

Did it capture a scream? Was there a scream?

Heavy footsteps climbed the stairs. My body swayed.

The house could swallow them too. *The bodies could rot there, they were no longer friends— they were a means to an end, and the house would collect them. Right? The same shadows I felt on my back, the crawling hands that locked me into the wall; they would splinter from the cellar door as the beast I recalled upstairs. Biting and tearing apart what was left on the floor with wide teeth and snapping jaws.*

I did not want to watch that. I didn't want to watch Hallie die either.

The walls carried me like snakes writhing over prey, twisting over my flesh and constricting my bones. I shut my eyes. I could suffocate here, inside the walls.

Watch.

I opened them again. I wasn't in the kitchen above the stairs. I was standing over Blake, seeing from my body's eyes again.

Twisting. Rug caught under dusty clothes, I would write. *Unable to escape.*

"Claire—please, what's going on?" Fat tears were gathered in Blake's eyes. They collected on his lashes when he blinked and fell away sideways to his ears. His voice cracked when he pleaded again, "Let me go, please—"

"—Sorry. I have to." I heard myself answer. The word cradled in my mouth, like a baby bird about to hatch. My arm strained, muscles tightened, locked to something. *Something*. It wet the sides of my fingers, but I did not let it go. Blake cried out again, but I could not move.

"Claire!" Again, he called my name. *Was I meant to answer? When I opened my mouth, would the cobwebs of the walls return? Or, perhaps they were spiderwebs, waiting for their escape to pour from my teeth in droves.* He continued to beg for my awareness, chorused with a steady lyric of 'no, no, no, no'.

He tried to crawl from under my knees. My body did not move. *Pinned by something. Watching. Writhing.*

In the back of my mind, or the depths of my muscle memory, familiarity twinged. *Leaves swirling above our heads and under our shoulders. Twisting and wrestling each other on the autumn lawn. Children's hands pinning each other down and missing tooth grins.*

"I'm— sorry. I'm sorry." Again, I heard the whispers spill between us. The knuckles holding the knife hilt grew tighter, but they did not pull or twist. We stayed as we were, my strength pushing against the last of his. "I have to get out, Blake."

His chest convulsed beneath me in response.

"I'm going to get famous, you're helping me become famous, that's what we wanted," I promised to the strands of hair stuck to his forehead. I could not look at his eyes, or how they frantically bulged from the sockets. "She's going to give me worth, I need this."

My words were swallowed by the guttural noises Blake made. He stopped twisting.

I needed this.

When I blinked, I was standing above Blake with the knife forgotten from my hands. It found a home within Blake's abdomen, coloring the pale hoodie he wore with a deep brown splotch. The computer had been on when I arrived in the room, but it now displayed slivers of my distorted form on a dead screen. I walked in on Blake clutching the device's corners. *Did he know?* I wondered if his nails indented the casing when I approached. *Unable to recall. It wouldn't matter now.*

In my article, I would write about how much I cared for him. How sincerely it affected me, how it stole the breath from my lungs and ripped desperate screams from me when the ghosts killed him.

I checked on Avery and Hallie downstairs after I heard Avery yell, and I found them dead with the knife. When I went to see Blake, the ghost had gotten to him too. I brought the knife with me, but I did not do it. I did not do it.

I did not do this. I was a witness to the house.

How long did I stand there?

The tendons in my hand ached from where the knife hilt pressed. The walls were still watching. *When I looked up, I would see them there— the eyes. Hundreds, stacked upon each other and blinking at my still frame. They watched my shoulders tremble and my feet stumble to the front door. My hesitant debate if I could just leave them, disappear into the soy fields, and begin to write of the horrors that happened between their faces— or if I should retreat to the mirror upstairs and confess my completion to the eyes in the glassy surface.*

I would tell her. She would reward me.

The house was still as my shoes rocked against the floor and up the stairs. No shadows followed me, no beasts at my ankles or blink of wallpaper. Silence fell over the bedroom, save for the squeak of the hinges as I opened the door. The mirror still lay abandoned in the closet. My knees framed it, and when I looked down— I frowned. The knees of my jeans had been soiled with russet. I pressed them on either side of the mirror before I lifted it in my palms, welcoming the smooth frame as cold water upon burns.

"I did it." I waited for her face to appear behind mine. The bare room reflected back. I looked into my own eyes again, assessing the life within them, and then to the room behind me. My face did not twist or morph, my hair fell against my forehead in a way I did not like— *where were my barrettes?* Sweat stuck on my eyebrow. I tapped the glass. Nothing appeared. "Am I worth it now?"

I waited.

No one came.

About the Author

Finch is a queer author writing queer stories. They dabble in fantasy, thriller, romance, and the occasional poem, striving to create stories emphasizing themes of tragedy and character relationships. When they aren't writing their problems away in a cafe somewhere, they enjoy reading outdoors, gaming, and telling their cat how lovely he is.

https://efinch.carrd.co

Printed in the USA
CPSIA information can be obtained
at www.ICGtesting.com
JSHW020300020923
47742JS00005BA/32